BETTER DEAD

By

J. M. BARRIE

Better Dead
by **J. M. Barrie**

ISBN: 978-93-57480-42-0

Published by

DOUBLE 9 BOOKS
2/13-B, Ansari Road
Daryaganj, New Delhi – 110002
info@double9books.com
www.double9books.com
Tel. 011-40042856

This book is under public domain

About The Author

Scottish author Sir James Matthew Barrie, 1st Baronet, is most known for creating Peter Pan. He was also a playwright. He was raised and educated in Scotland before relocating to London, where he penned a number of well-received books and plays. There, he met the Llewelyn Davies brothers, who later served as the inspiration for his works Peter Pan, or The Boy Who Wouldn't Grow Up, a 1904 West End "fairy play," about an ageless boy and an ordinary girl named Wendy who have adventures in the fantasy setting of Neverland. The story of a baby boy who has magical adventures in Kensington Gardens was first included in Barrie's 1902 adult novel The Little White Bird. Despite his ongoing success as a writer, Peter Pan eclipsed all of his earlier works and is credited with making the name Wendy well-known. After the deaths of the Davies boys' parents, Barrie adopted them clandestinely. George V created Barrie a baronet on June 14, 1913, and in the New Year's Honours of 1922, he was inducted into the Order of Merit.

CONTENTS

INTRODUCTION

This is the only American edition of my books produced with my sanction, and I have special reasons for thanking Messrs. Scribner for its publication; they let it be seen, by this edition, what are my books, for I know not how many volumes purporting to be by me, are in circulation in America which are no books of mine. I have seen several of these, bearing such titles as "Two of Them," "An Auld Licht Manse," "A Tillyloss Scandal," and some of them announce themselves as author's editions, or published by arrangement with the author. They consist of scraps collected and published without my knowledge, and I entirely disown them. I have written no books save those that appear in this edition.

I am asked to write a few lines on the front page of each of these volumes, to say something, as I take it, about how they came into being. Well, they were written mainly to please one woman who is now dead, but as I am writing a little book about my mother I shall say no more of her here.

Many of the chapters in "Auld Licht Idylls" first appeared in a different form in the St. James's Gazette , and there is little doubt that they would never have appeared anywhere but for the encouragement given to me by the editor of that paper. It was pressure from him that induced me to write a second "Idyll" and a third after I thought the first completed the picture, he set me thinking seriously of these people, and though he knew nothing of them himself, may be said to have led me back to them. It seems odd, and yet I am not the first nor the fiftieth who has left Thrums at sunrise to seek the life-work that was all the time awaiting him at home. And we seldom sally forth a second time. I had always meant to be a novelist, but London, I thought, was the quarry.

For long I had an uneasy feeling that no one save the editor read my contributions, for I was leading a lonely life in London, and not another editor could I find in the land willing to print the Scotch dialect. The magazines, Scotch and English, would have nothing to say to me--I think I tried them all with "The Courting of T'nowhead's Bell," but it never found shelter until it got within book-covers. In time, however, I found another paper, the British

Weekly , with an editor as bold as my first (or shall we say he suffered from the same infirmity?). He revived my drooping hopes, and I was again able to turn to the only kind of literary work I now seemed to have much interest in. He let me sign my articles, which was a big step for me and led to my having requests for work from elsewhere, but always the invitations said "not Scotch--the public will not read dialect." By this time I had put together from these two sources and from my drawerful of rejected stories this book of "Auld Licht Idylls," and in its collected form it again went the rounds. I offered it to certain firms as a gift, but they would not have it even at that. And then, on a day came actually an offer for it from Messrs. Hodder and Stoughton. For this, and for many another kindness, I had the editor of the British Weekly to thank. Thus the book was published at last, and as for Messrs. Hodder and Stoughton I simply dare not say what a generous firm I found them, lest it send too many aspirants to their doors. But, indeed, I have had the pleasantest relations with all my publishers.

"Better Dead" is, by my wish, no longer on sale in Great Britain, and I should have preferred not to see it here, for it is in no way worthy of the beautiful clothes Messrs. Scribner have given it. Weighted with "An Edinburgh Eleven" it would rest very comfortably in the mill dam, but the publishers have reasons for its inclusion; among them, I suspect, is a well-grounded fear that if I once began to hack and hew, I should not stop until I had reduced the edition to two volumes. This juvenile effort is a field of prickles into which none may be advised to penetrate--I made the attempt lately in cold blood and came back shuddering, but I had read enough to have the profoundest reason for declining to tell what the book is about. And yet I have a sentimental interest in "Better Dead," for it was my first--published when I had small hope of getting any one to accept the Scotch--and there was a week when I loved to carry it in my pocket and did not think it dead weight. Once I almost saw it find a purchaser. She was a pretty girl and it lay on a bookstall, and she read some pages and smiled, and then retired, and came back and began another chapter. Several times she did this, and I stood in the background trembling with hope and fear. At last she went away without the book, but I am still of opinion that, had it been just a little bit better, she would have bought it.

CHAPTER I

When Andrew Riach went to London, his intention was to become private secretary to a member of the Cabinet. If time permitted, he proposed writing for the Press.

"It might be better if you and Clarrie understood each other," the minister said.

It was their last night together. They faced each other in the manse-parlour at Wheens, whose low, peeled ceiling had threatened Mr. Eassie at his desk every time he looked up with his pen in his mouth until his wife died, when he ceased to notice things. The one picture on the walls, an engraving of a boy in velveteen, astride a tree, entitled "Boyhood of Bunyan," had started life with him. The horsehair chairs were not torn, and you did not require to know the sofa before you sat down on it, that day thirty years before, when a chubby minister and his lady walked to the manse between two cart-loads of furniture, trying not to look elated.

Clarrie rose to go, when she heard her name. The love-light was in her eyes, but Andrew did not open the door for her, for he was a Scotch graduate. Besides, she might one day be his wife.

The minister's toddy-ladle clinked against his tumbler, but Andrew did not speak. Clarrie was the girl he generally adored.

"As for Clarrie," he said at last, "she puts me in an awkward position. How do I know that I love her?"

"You have known each other a long time," said the minister.

His guest was cleaning his pipe with a hair-pin, that his quick eye had detected on the carpet.

"And she is devoted to you," continued Mr. Eassie.

The young man nodded.

"What I fear," he said, "is that we have known each other too long. Perhaps my feeling for Clarrie is only brotherly--"

"Hers for you, Andrew, is more than sisterly."

"Admitted. But consider, Mr. Eassie, she has only seen the world in soirées. Every girl has her day-dreams, and Clarrie has perhaps made a dream of me. She is impulsive, given to idealisation, and hopelessly illogical."

The minister moved uneasily in his chair.

"I have reasoned out her present relation to me," the young man went on, "and, the more you reduce it to the usual formulae, the more illogical it becomes. Clarrie could possibly describe me, but define me--never. What is our prospect of happiness in these circumstances?"

"But love--" began Mr. Eassie.

"Love!" exclaimed Andrew. "Is there such a thing? Reduce it to syllogistic form, and how does it look in Barbara?"

For the moment there was almost some expression in his face, and he suffered from a determination of words to the mouth.

"Love and logic," Mr. Eassie interposed, "are hardly kindred studies."

"Is love a study at all?" asked Andrew, bitterly. "It is but the trail of idleness. But all idleness is folly; therefore, love is folly."

Mr. Eassie was not so keen a logician as his guest, but he had age for a major premiss. He was easy-going rather than a coward; a preacher who, in the pulpit, looked difficulties genially in the face, and passed them by.

Riach had a very long neck. He was twenty-five years of age, fair, and somewhat heavily built, with a face as inexpressive as book-covers.

A native of Wheens and an orphan, he had been brought up by his uncle, who was a weaver and read Herodotus in the original. The uncle starved himself to buy books and talk about them, until one day he got a good meal, and died of it. Then Andrew apprenticed himself to a tailor.

When his time was out, he walked fifty miles to Aberdeen University, and got a bursary. He had been there a month, when his professor said good-naturedly--

"Don't you think, Mr. Riach, you would get on better if you took your hands out of your pockets?"

"No, sir, I don't think so," replied Andrew, in all honesty.

When told that he must apologise, he did not see it, but was willing to argue the matter out.

Next year he matriculated at Edinburgh, sharing one room with two others; studying through the night, and getting their bed when they rose. He was a failure in the classics, because they left you where you were, but in his third year he woke the logic class-room, and frightened the professor of moral philosophy.

He was nearly rusticated for praying at a debating society for a divinity professor who was in the chair.

"O Lord!" he cried, fervently, "open his eyes, guide his tottering footsteps, and lead him from the paths of folly into those that are lovely and of good report, for lo! his days are numbered, and the sickle has been sharpened, and the corn is not yet ripe for the cutting."

When Andrew graduated he was known as student of mark.

He returned to Wheens, before setting out for London, with the consciousness of his worth.

Yet he was only born to follow, and his chance of making a noise in the world rested on his meeting a stronger than himself. During his summer vacations he had weaved sufficient money to keep himself during the winter on porridge and potatoes.

Clarrie was beautiful and all that.

"We'll say no more about it, then," the minister said after a pause.

"The matter," replied Andrew, "cannot be dismissed in that way. Reasonable or not, I do undoubtedly experience sensations similar to Clarrie's. But in my love I notice a distinct ebb and flow. There are times when I don't care a hang for her."

"Andrew!"

"I beg your pardon. Still, it is you who have insisted on discussing this question in the particular instance. Love in the abstract is of much greater moment."

"I have sometimes thought, Andrew," Mr. Eassie said, "that you are lacking in the imaginative faculty."

"In other words, love is a mere fancy. Grant that, and see to what it leads. By imagining that I have Clarrie with me I am as well off as if I really had. Why, then, should I go to needless expense, and take her from you?"

The white-haired minister rose, for the ten o'clock bell was ringing and it was time for family worship.

"My boy," he said, "if there must be a sacrifice let the old man make it. I, too, have imagination."

For the moment there was a majesty about him that was foreign to his usual bearing. Andrew was touched, and gripped his hand.

"Rather," he cried, "let the girl we both love remain with you. She will be here waiting for me--should I return."

"More likely," said the minister, "she will be at the bank."

The banker was unmarried, and had once in February and again in June seen Clarrie home from the Dorcas Society. The town talked about it. Strictly speaking, gentlemen should not attend these meetings; but in Wheens there was not much difference between the men and the women.

That night, as Clarrie bade Andrew farewell at the garden gate, he took her head in his hands and asked what this talk about the banker meant.

It was no ignoble curiosity that prompted him. He would rather have got engaged to her there and then than have left without feeling sure of her.

His sweetheart looked her reply straight his eyes.

"Andrew!" was all she said.

It was sufficient. He knew that he did not require to press his point.

Lover's watches stand still. At last Andrew stooped and kissed her upturned face.

"If a herring and a half," he said anxiously, "cost three half-pence, how many will you get for elevenpence?"

Clarrie was mute.

Andrew shuddered; he felt that he was making a mistake.

"Why do I kiss you?" he cried. "What good does it do either of us?"

He looked fiercely at his companion, and her eyes filled with tears.

"Where even is the pleasure in it?" he added brutally.

The only objectionable thing about Clarrie was her long hair.

She wore a black frock and looked very breakable. Nothing irritates a man so much.

Andrew gathered her passionately in his arms, while a pained, puzzled expression struggled to reach his face.

Then he replaced her roughly on the ground and left her.

It was impossible to say whether they were engaged.

CHAPTER II

Andrew reached King's Cross on the following Wednesday morning.

It was the first time he had set foot in England, and he naturally thought of Bannockburn.

He left his box in the cloak-room, and, finding his way into Bloomsbury, took a bed-room at the top of a house in Bernard Street.

Then he returned for his box, carried it on his back to his lodgings, and went out to buy a straw hat. It had not struck him to be lonely.

He bought two pork pies in an eating-house in Gray's Inn Road, and set out for Harley Street, looking at London on the way.

Mr. Gladstone was at home, but all his private secretaryships were already filled.

Andrew was not greatly disappointed, though he was too polite to say so. In politics he was a granite-headed Radical; and on several questions, such as the Church and Free Education, the two men were hopelessly at variance.

Mr. Chamberlain was the man with whom, on the whole, he believed it would be best to work. But Mr. Chamberlain could not even see him.

Looking back to this time, it is impossible not to speculate upon how things might have turned out had the Radical party taken Andrew to them in his day of devotion to their cause.

This is the saddest spectacle in life, a brave young man's first meeting with the world. How rapidly the milk turns to gall! For the cruellest of his acts the vivisectionist has not even the excuse that science benefits.

Here was a young Scotchman, able, pure, of noble ambition, and a first medallist in metaphysics. Genius was written on his brow. He may have written it himself, but it was there.

He offered to take a pound a week less than any other secretary in London. Not a Cabinet Minister would have him. Lord Randolph Churchill would not speak to him. He had fifty-eight testimonials with him. They would neither read nor listen to them.

He could not fasten a quarrel on London, for it never recognised his existence. What a commentary on our vaunted political life!

Andrew tried the Press.

He sent one of the finest things that was ever written on the Ontology of Being to paper after paper, and it was never used. He threatened the "Times" with legal proceedings if it did not return the manuscript.

The "Standard" sent him somebody else's manuscript, and seemed to think it would do as well.

In a fortnight his enthusiasm had been bled to death.

His testimonials were his comfort and his curse. He would have committed suicide without them, but they kept him out of situations.

He had the fifty-eight by heart, and went over them to himself all day. He fell asleep with them, and they were there when he woke.

The moment he found himself in a great man's presence he began:

"From the Rev. Peter Mackay, D. D., author of 'The Disruption Divines,' Minister of Free St. King's, Dundee.--I have much pleasure in stating that I have known Mr. Andrew Gordon Cummings Riach for many years, and have been led to form a high opinion of his ability. In the summer of 18-- Mr. Riach had entire charge of a class in my Sabbath school, when I had ample opportunity of testing his efficiency, unwearying patience, exceptional power of illustration and high Christian character," and so on.

Or he might begin at the beginning:

"Testimonials in favour of Andrew G. C. Riach, M.A. (Edin.), applicant for the post of Private Secretary to any one of her Majesty's Cabinet Ministers, 6 Candlish Street, Wheens, N. B.--I, Andrew G. C. Riach, beg to offer myself as a candidate for the post of private secretary, and submit the following testimonials in my favour for your consideration. I am twenty-five years of age, a Master of Arts of the University of Edinburgh, and a member of the Free Church of Scotland. At the University I succeeded in carrying a bursary of 14 l. 10 s. per annum, tenable for four years. I was first medallist in the class of Logic and Metaphysics, thirteenth prizeman in Mathematics, and had a certificate of merit in the class of Natural Philosophy, as will be seen from my testimonials."

However, he seldom got as far as this.

It was when alone that these testimonials were his truest solace. Had you met him in the Strand conning them over, you might have taken him for an actor. He had a yearning to stop strangers in the streets and try a testimonial's effect on them.

Every young man is not equally unfortunate.

Riach's appearance was against him.

There was a suggestion of latent strength about him that made strangers uncomfortable. Even the friends who thought they understood him liked him to go away.

Lord Rosebery made several jokes to him, and Andrew only looked at him in response. The general feeling was that he was sneering at you somewhere in his inside.

Let us do no one an injustice.

As it turned out, the Cabinet and Press were but being used in this case as the means to an end.

A grand work lay ready for Andrew's hand when he was fit to perform it, but he had to learn Naked Truth first. It was ordained that they should teach it him. Providence sometimes makes use of strange instruments.

Riach had two pounds with him when he came to London, and in a month they had almost gone.

Now and again he made an odd five shillings.

Do you know how men in his position live in London?

He could not afford the profession of not having any.

At one time he was a phrasemonger for politicians, especially for the Irish members, who were the only ones that paid.

Some of his phrases have become Parliamentary. Thus "Buckshot" was his. "Mend them--End them," "Grand Old Man," and "Legislation by Picnic" may all be traced to the struggling young man from Wheens.[1]

He supplied the material for obituary notices.

When the newspaper placards announced the serious illness of a distinguished man, he made up characteristic anecdotes about his childhood, his reputation at school, his first love, and sent them as the reminiscences of a friend to the great London dailies. These were the only things of his they used. As often as not the invalid got better, and then Andrew went without a dinner.

Once he offered his services to a Conservative statesman; at another time he shot himself in the coat in Northumberland Street, Strand, to oblige an evening paper (five shillings).

He fainted in the pit of a theatre to the bribe of an emotional tragedian (a guinea).

He assaulted a young lady and her aunt with a view to robbery, in a quiet thoroughfare, by arrangement with a young gentleman, who rescued them and made him run (ten shillings).

It got into the papers that he had fled from the wax policeman at Tussaud's (half-a-crown).

More than once he sold his body in advance to the doctors, and was never able to buy it out.[2]

It would be a labour, thankless as impossible, to recover now all the devices by which Andrew disgraced his manhood during these weeks rather than die. As well count the "drinks" an actor has in a day.

It is not our part to climb down into the depths after him. He re-appeared eventually, or this record would never have been written.

During this period of gloom, Clarrie wrote him frequently long and tender epistles.

More strictly, the minister wrote them, for he had the gift of beautiful sentiment in letters, which had been denied to her.

She copied them, however, and signed them, and they were a great consolation.

The love of a good girl is a priceless possession, or rather, in this case, of a good minister.

So long as you do not know which, it does not make much difference.

At times Andrew's reason may have been unhinged, less on account of his reverses than because no one spoke to him.

There were days and nights when he rushed all over London.

In the principal streets the stolid-faced Scotchman in a straw hat became a familiar figure.

Strange fancies held him. He stood for an hour at a time looking at his face in a shop-window.

The boot-blacks pointed at him and he disappeared down passages.

He shook his fist at the 'bus-conductors, who would not leave him alone.

In the yellow night policemen drew back scared, as he hurried past them on his way to nowhere.

In the day-time Oxford Street was his favourite thoroughfare. He was very irritable at this time, and could not leave his fellow wayfarers alone.

More than once he poked his walking-stick through the eyeglass of a brave young gentleman.

He would turn swiftly round to catch people looking at him.

When a small boy came in his way, he took him by the neck and planted him on the curb-stone.

If a man approached simpering, Andrew stopped and gazed at him. The smile went from the stranger's face; he blushed or looked fierce. When he turned round, Andrew still had his eye on him. Sometimes he came bouncing back.

"What are you so confoundedly happy about?" Andrew asked.

When he found a crowd gazing in at a "while you wait" shop-window, or entranced over the paving of a street--

"Splendid, isn't it?" he said to the person nearest him.

He dropped a penny, which he could ill spare, into the hat of an exquisite who annoyed him by his way of lifting it to a lady.

When he saw a man crossing the street too daintily, he ran after him and hit him over the legs.

Even on his worst days his reasoning powers never left him. Once a mother let her child slip from her arms to the pavement.

She gave a shriek.

"My good woman," said Andrew, testily, "what difference can one infant in the world more or less make?"

We come now to an eccentricity, engendered of loneliness, that altered the whole course of his life. Want had battered down his door. Truth had been evolved from despair. He was at last to have a flash into salvation.

To give an object to his walks abroad he would fasten upon a wayfarer and follow him till he ran him to his destination. Chance led to his selecting one quarry rather than another. He would dog a man's footsteps, struck by the glossiness of his boots, or to discover what he was in such a hurry about, or merely because he had a good back to follow. Probably he seldom knew what attracted him, and sometimes when he realised the pursuit he gave it up.

On these occasions there was one person only who really interested him. This was a man, somewhat over middle age, of singularly noble and distinguished bearing. His brow was furrowed with lines, but they spoke of cares of the past. Benevolence had settled on his face. It was as if, after a weary struggle, the sun had broken through the heavy clouds. He was attired in the ordinary dress of an English gentleman; but once, when he raised his head to see if it rained, Andrew noticed that he only wore a woollen shirt, without a necktie. As a rule, his well-trimmed, venerable beard hid this from view.

He seemed a man of unostentatious means. Andrew lost him in Drury Lane and found him again in Piccadilly. He was generally alone, never twice with the same person. His business was scattered, or it was his pleasure that kept him busy. He struck the observer as always being on the outlook for someone who did not come.

Why attempt to account for the nameless fascination he exercised over the young Scotchman? We speak lightly of mesmeric influence, but, after all, there is only one mesmerist for youth--a good woman or a good man. Depend upon it, that is why so many "mesmerists" have mistaken their vocation. Andrew took to prowling about the streets looking for this man, like a dog that has lost its master.

The day came when they met.

Andrew was returning from the Crystal Palace, which he had been viewing from the outside. He had walked both ways. Just as he rounded the upper end of Chancery Lane, a man walking rapidly struck against him, whirled him aside, and hurried on.

The day was done, but as yet the lamps only dimmed the streets.

Andrew had been dreaming, and the jerk woke him to the roar of London.

It was as if he had taken his fingers from his ears.

He staggered, dazed, against a 'bus-horse, but the next moment he was in pursuit of the stranger. It was but a continuation of his dream. He felt that something was about to happen. He had never seen this man disturbed before.

Chancery Lane swarmed with lawyers, but if they had not made way Andrew would have walked over them.

He clove his way between those walking abreast, and struck down an arm extended to point out the Law Courts. When he neared the stranger, he slightly slackened his pace, but it was a stampede even then.

Suddenly the pursued came to a dead stop and gazed for twenty minutes in at a pastry-cook's window. Andrew waited for him. Then they started off again, much more leisurely.

They turned Chancery Lane almost together. All this time Andrew had failed to catch sight of the other's face.

He stopped twice in the Strand for a few minutes.

At Charing Cross he seemed for a moment at a loss. Then he sprang across the street, and went back the way he came.

It was now for the first time that a strange notion illumined Andrew's brain. It bewildered him, and left him in darkness the next moment. But his blood was running hot now, and his eyes were glassy.

They turned down Arundel Street.

It was getting dark. There were not a dozen people in the narrow thoroughfare.

His former thought leapt back into Andrew's mind--not a fancy now, but a fact. The stranger was following someone too.

For what purpose? His own?

Andrew did not put the question to himself.

There were not twenty yards between the three of them.

What Riach saw in front was a short stout man proceeding cheerfully down the street. He delayed in a doorway to light a cigar, and the stranger stopped as if turned to stone.

Andrew stopped too.

They were like the wheels of a watch. The first wheel moved on, and set the others going again.

For a hundred yards or more they walked in procession in a westerly direction without meeting a human being. At last the first of the trio half turned on his heel and leant over the Embankment.

Riach drew back into the shade, just before the stranger took a lightning glance behind him.

The young man saw his face now. It was never fuller of noble purpose; yet why did Andrew cry out?

The next moment the stranger had darted forward, slipped his arms round the little man's legs, and toppled him into the river.

There was a splash but no shriek.

Andrew bounded forward, but the stranger held him by one hand. His clear blue eyes looked down a little wistfully upon the young Scotchman, who never felt the fascination of a master-mind more than at that moment. As if feeling his power, the elder man relaxed his hold and pointed to the spot where his victim had disappeared.

"He was a good man," he said, more to himself than to Andrew, "and the world has lost a great philanthropist; but he is better as he is."

Then he lifted a paving-stone, and peered long and earnestly into the waters.

The short stout man, however, did not rise again.

[1] Some time afterwards Lord Rosebery convulsed an audience by a story about a friend of his who complained that you get "no forrarder" on claret. Andrew was that friend.

[2] He had fine ideas, but no money to work them out. One was to start a serious "Spectator," on the lines of the present one, but not so flippant and frivolous.

CHAPTER III

Lost in reverie, the stranger stood motionless on the Embankment. The racket of the city was behind him. At his feet lay a drowned world, its lights choking in the Thames. It was London, as it will be on the last day.

With an effort he roused himself and took Andrew's arm.

"The body will soon be recovered," he said, in a voice of great dejection, "and people will talk. Let us go."

They retraced their steps up Arundel Street.

"Now," said Andrew's companion, "tell me who you are."

Andrew would have preferred to hear who the stranger was. In the circumstances he felt that he had almost a right to know. But this was not a man to brook interference.

"If you will answer me one question," the young Scotchman said humbly, "I shall tell you everything."

His reveries had made Andrew quick-witted, and he had the judicial mind which prevents one's judging another rashly. Besides, his hankering after this man had already suggested an exculpation for him.

"You are a Radical?" he asked eagerly.

The stranger's brows contracted. "Young man," he said, "though all the Radicals, and Liberals, and Conservatives who ever addressed the House of Commons were in ----, I would not stoop to pick them up, though I could gather them by the gross."

He said this without an Irish accent, and Andrew felt that he had better begin his story at once.

He told everything.

As his tale neared its conclusion his companion scanned him narrowly.

If the stranger's magnanimous countenance did not beam down in sympathy upon the speaker, it was because surprise and gratification filled it.

Only once an ugly look came into his eyes. That was when Andrew had reached the middle of his second testimonial.

The young man saw the look, and at the same time felt the hold on his arm become a grip.

His heart came into his mouth. He gulped it down, and, with what was perhaps a judicious sacrifice, jumped the remainder of his testimonials.

When the stranger heard how he had been tracked through the streets, he put his head to the side to think.

It was a remarkable compliment to his abstraction that Andrew paused involuntarily in his story and waited.

He felt that his future was in the balance. Those sons of peers may faintly realise his position whose parents have hesitated whether to make statesmen or cattle-dealers of them.

"I don't mind telling you," the stranger said at last, "that your case has been under consideration. When we left the Embankment my intention was to dispose of you in a doorway. But your story moves me strangely. Could I be certain that you felt the sacredness of human life--as I fear no boy can feel it--I should be tempted to ask you instead to become one of us."

There was something in this remark about the sacredness of human life that was not what Andrew expected, and his answer died unspoken.

"Youth," continued the stranger, "is enthusiasm, but not enthusiasm in a straight line. We are impotent in directing it, like a boy with a toy engine. How carefully the child sets it off, how soon it goes off the rails! So youth is wrecked. The slightest obstacle sends it off at a tangent. The vital force expended in a wrong direction does evil instead of good. You know the story of Atalanta. It has always been misread. She was the type not of woman but of youth, and Hippomenes personated age. He was the slower runner, but he won the race; and yet how beautiful, even where it run to riot, must enthusiasm be in such a cause as ours!"

"If Atalanta had been Scotch," said Andrew "she would not have lost that race for a pound of apples."

The stranger regarded him longingly, like a father only prevented by state reasons from embracing his son.

He murmured something that Andrew hardly caught.

It sounded like:

"Atalanta would have been better dead."

"Your nationality is in your favour," he said, "and you have served your apprenticeship to our calling. You have been tending towards us ever since you came to London. You are an apple ripe for plucking, and if you are not plucked now you will fall. I would fain take you by the hand, and yet--"

"And yet?"

"And yet I hesitate. You seem a youth of the fairest promise; but how often have I let these impulses deceive me! You talk of logic, but is it more than talk? Man, they say, is a reasonable being. They are wrong. He is only a being capable of reason."

"Try me," said Andrew.

The stranger resumed in a lower key:

"You do not understand what you ask as yet," he said; "still less what we would ask in return of you."

"I have seen something to-day," said Andrew.

"But you are mistaken in its application. You think I followed the man lately deceased as pertinaciously as you followed me. You are wrong. When you met me in Chancery Lane I was in pursuit of a gentleman to whose case I have devoted myself for several days. It has interested me much. There is no reason why I should conceal his name. It is one honoured in this country, Sir Wilfrid Lawson. He looked in on his man of business, which delayed me at the shop-window of which you have spoken. I waited for him, and I thought I had him this time. But you see I lost him in the Strand, after all."

"But the other, then," Andrew asked, "who was he?"

"Oh, I picked him up at Charing Cross. He was better dead."

"I think," said Andrew, hopefully, "that my estimate of the sacredness of human life is sufficiently high for your purpose. If that is the only point--"

"Ah, they all say that until they join. I remember an excellent young man who came among us for a time. He seemed discreet beyond his years, and we expected great things of him. But it was the old story. For young men the cause is as demoralizing as boarding schools are for girls."

"What did he do?"

"It went to his head. He took a bedroom in Pall Mall and sat at the window with an electric rifle picking them off on the door-steps of the clubs. It was a noble idea, but of course it imperilled the very existence of the society. He was a curate."

"What became of him?" asked Andrew.

"He is better dead," said the stranger, softly.

"And the Society you speak of, what is it?"

"The S. D. W. S. P."

"The S. D. W. S. P.?"

"Yes, the Society for Doing Without Some People."

They were in Holborn, but turned up Southampton Row for quiet.

"You have told me," said the stranger, now speaking rapidly, "that at times you have felt tempted to take your life, that life for which you will one day have to account. Suicide is the coward's refuge. You are miserable? When a young man knows that, he is happy. Misery is but preparing for an old age of delightful reminiscence. You say that London has no work for you, that the functions to which you looked forward are everywhere discharged by another. That need not drive you to despair. If it proves that someone should die, does it necessarily follow that the someone is you?"

"But is not the other's life as sacred as mine?"

"That is his concern."

"Then you would have me--"

"Certainly not. You are a boxer without employment, whom I am showing what to hit. In such a case as yours the Society would be represented by a third party, whose decision would be final. As an interested person you would have to stand aside."

"I don't understand."

"The arbitrator would settle if you should go."

Andrew looked blank.

"Go?" he repeated.

"It is a euphemism for die," said his companion a little impatiently. "This is a trivial matter, and hardly worth going into at any length. It shows our process, however, and the process reveals the true character of the organization. As I have already mentioned, the Society takes for its first principle the sanctity of human life. Everyone who has mixed much among his fellow-creatures must be aware that this is adulterated, so to speak, by numbers of spurious existences. Many of these are a nuisance to themselves. Others may at an earlier period have been lives of great promise and fulfilment. In the case of the latter, how sad to think that they should be dragged out into worthlessness or dishonour, all for want of a friendly hand to snap them short! In the lower form of life the process of preying upon animals whose work is accomplished--that is, of weeding--goes on continually. Man must, of course, be more cautious. The grand function of the Society is to find out the persons who have a claim on it, and in the interests of humanity to lay their condition before them. After that it is in the majority of cases for themselves to decide whether they will go or stay on."

"But," said Andrew, "had the gentleman in the Thames consented to go?"

"No, that was a case where assistance had to be given. He had been sounded, though."

"And do you find," asked Andrew, "that many of them are--agreeable?"

"I admit," said the stranger, "that so far that has been our chief difficulty. Even the men we looked upon as certainties have fallen short of our expectations. There is Mallock, now, who said that life was not worth living. I called on him only last week, fully expecting him to meet me half-way."

"And he didn't?"

"Mallock was a great disappointment," said the stranger, with genuine pain in his voice.

He liked Mallock.

"However," he added, brightening, "his case comes up for hearing at the next meeting. If I have two-thirds of the vote we proceed with it."

"But how do the authorities take it?" asked Andrew.

"Pooh!" said the stranger.

Andrew, however, could not think so.

"It is against the law, you know," he said.

"The law winks at it," the stranger said. "Law has its feelings as well as we. We have two London magistrates and a minister on the executive, and the Lord Chief Justice is an honorary member."

Andrew raised his eyes.

"This, of course, is private," continued the stranger. "These men join on the understanding that if anything comes out they deny all connection with us. But they have the thing at heart. I have here a very kind letter from Gladstone--"

He felt in his pockets.

"I seem to have left it at home. However, its purport was that he hoped we would not admit Lord Salisbury an honorary member."

"Why not?"

"Well, the Society has power to take from its numbers, so far as ordinary members are concerned, but it is considered discourteous to reduce the honorary list."

"Then why have honorary members?" asked Andrew in a burst of enthusiasm.

"It is a necessary precaution. They subscribe largely too. Indeed, the association is now established on a sound commercial basis. We are paying six per cent."

"None of these American preachers who come over to this country are honorary members?" asked Andrew, anxiously.

"No; one of them made overtures to us, but we would not listen to him. Why?"

"Oh, nothing," said Andrew.

"To do the honorary list justice," said his companion, "it gave us one fine fellow in our honorary president. He is dead now."

Andrew looked up.

"No, we had nothing to do with it. It was Thomas Carlyle."

Andrew raised his hat.

"Though he was over eighty years of age," continued the stranger. "Carlyle would hardly rest content with merely giving us his countenance. He wanted to be a working member. It was he who mentioned Froude's name to us."

"For honorary membership?"

"Not at all. Froude would hardly have completed the 'Reminiscences' had it not been that we could never make up our minds between him and Freeman."

Youth is subject to sudden fits of despondency. Its hopes go up and down like a bucket in a draw-well.

"They'll never let me join," cried Andrew, sorrowfully.

His companion pressed his hand.

"Three black balls exclude," he said, "but you have the president on your side. With my introduction you will be admitted a probationer, and after that everything depends on yourself."

"I thought you must be the president from the first," said Andrew, reverently.

He had not felt so humble since the first day he went to the University and walked past and repast it, frightened to go in.

"How long," he asked, "does the period of probation last?"

"Three months. Then you send in a thesis, and if it is considered satisfactory you become a member."

"And if it isn't?"

The president did not say.

"A thesis," he said, "is generally a paper with a statement of the line of action you propose to adopt, subject to the Society's approval. Each member has his specialty--as law, art, divinity, literature, and the like."

"Does the probationer devote himself exclusively during these three months to his thesis?"

"On the contrary, he never has so much liberty as at this period. He is expected to be practising."

"Practising?"

"Well, experimenting, getting his hand in, so to speak. The member acts under instructions only, but the probationer just does what he thinks best."

"There is a man on my stair," said Andrew, after a moment's consideration, "who asks his friends in every Friday night, and recites to them with his door open. I think I should like to begin with him."

"As a society we do not recognise these private cases. The public gain is so infinitesimal. We had one probationer who constructed a very ingenious water-butt for boys. Another had a scheme for clearing the streets of the people who get in the way. He got into trouble about some perambulators. Let me see your hands."

They stopped at a lamp-post.

"They are large, which is an advantage," said the president, fingering Andrew's palms; "but are they supple?"

Andrew had thought very little about it, and he did not quite comprehend.

"The hands," explained the president, "are perhaps the best natural weapon; but, of course, there are different ways of doing it."

The young Scotchman's brain, however, could not keep pace with his companion's words, and the president looked about him for an illustration.

They stopped at Gower Street station and glanced at the people coming out.

None of them was of much importance, but the president left them alone.

Andrew saw what he meant now, and could not but admire his forbearance.

They turned away, but just as they emerged into the blaze of Tottenham Court Road they ran into two men, warmly shaking hands with each other before they parted. One of them wore an eye-glass.

"Chamberlain!" exclaimed the president, rushing after him.

"Did you recognise the other?" said Andrew, panting at his heels.

"No! who was it?"

"Stead, of the 'Pall Mall Gazette.'"

"Great God," cried the president, "two at a time!"

He turned and ran back. Then he stopped irresolutely. He could not follow the one for thought of the other.

CHAPTER IV

The London cabman's occupation consists in dodging thoroughfares under repair.

Numbers of dingy streets have been flung about to help him. There is one of these in Bloomsbury, which was originally discovered by a student while looking for the British Museum. It runs a hundred yards in a straight line, then stops, like a stranger who has lost his way, and hurries by another route out of the neighbourhood.

The houses are dull, except one, just where it doubles, which is gloomy.

This house is divided into sets of chambers and has a new frontage, but it no longer lets well. A few years ago there were two funerals from it within a fortnight, and soon afterward another of the tenants was found at the foot of the stair with his neck broken. These fatalities gave the house a bad name, as such things do in London.

It was here that Andrew's patron, the president, lived.

To the outcast from work to get an object in life is to be born again. Andrew bustled to the president's chambers on the Saturday night following the events already described, with his chest well set.

His springy step echoed of wages in the hearts of the unemployed. Envious eyes, following his swaggering staff, could not see that but a few days before he had been as the thirteenth person at a dinner-party.

Such a change does society bring about when it empties a chair for the superfluous man.

It may be wondered that he felt so sure of himself, for the night had still to decide his claims.

Andrew, however, had thought it all out in his solitary lodgings, and had put fear from him. He felt his failings and allowed for every one of them, but he knew his merits too, and his testimonials were in his pocket. Strength of purpose was his weak point, and, though the good of humanity was his loadstar, it did not make him quite forget self.

It may not be possible to serve both God and mammon, but since Adam the world has been at it. We ought to know by this time.

The Society for Doing Without was as immoral as it certainly was illegal. The president's motives were not more disinterested than his actions were defensible. He even deserved punishment.

All these things may be. The great social question is not to be solved in a day. It never will be solved if those who take it by the beard are not given an unbiassed hearing.

Those were the young Scotchman's views when the president opened the door to him, and what he saw and heard that night strengthened them.

It was characteristic of Andrew's host that at such a time he could put himself in the young man's place.

He took his hand and looked him in the face more like a physician than a mere acquaintance. Then he drew him aside into an empty room.

"Let me be the first to congratulate you," he said; "you are admitted."

Andrew took a long breath, and the president considerately turned away his head until the young probationer had regained his composure. Then he proceeded:

"The society only asks from its probationers the faith which it has in them. They take no oath. We speak in deeds. The Brotherhood do not recognise the possibility of treachery; but they are prepared to cope with it if it comes. Better far, Andrew Riach, to be in your grave, dead and rotten and forgotten, than a traitor to the cause."

The president's voice trembled with solemnity.

He stretched forth his hands, slowly repeating the words, "dead and rotten and forgotten," until his wandering eyes came to rest on the young man's neck.

Andrew drew back a step and bowed silently, as he had seen many a father do at a christening in the kirk at Wheens.

"You will shortly," continued the president, with a return to his ordinary manner, "hear an address on female suffrage from one of the noblest women in the land. It will be your part to listen. To-night you will both hear and see strange things. Say nothing. Evince no surprise. Some members are irritable. Come!"

Once more he took Andrew by the hand, and led him into the meeting-room; and still his eyes were fixed on the probationer's neck. There seemed to be something about it that he liked.

It was not then, with the committee all around him, but long afterwards at Wheens, that Andrew was struck by the bareness of the chambers.

Without the president's presence they had no character.

The trifles were absent that are to a room what expression is to the face.

The tenant might have been a medical student who knew that it was not worth while to unpack his boxes.

The only ornament on the walls was an elaborate sketch by a member, showing the arrangement of the cellars beneath the premises of the Young Men's Christian Association.

There were a dozen men in the room, including the president of the Birmingham branch association and two members who had just returned from a visit to Edinburgh. These latter had already submitted their report.

The president introduced Andrew to the committee, but not the committee to him. Several of them he recognized from the portraits in the shop windows.

They stood or sat in groups looking over a probationer's thesis. It consisted of diagrams of machinery.

Andrew did not see the sketches, though they were handed round separately for inspection, but he listened eagerly to the president's explanations.

"The first," said the president, "is a beautiful little instrument worked by steam. Having placed his head on the velvet cushion D, the subject can confidently await results.

"No. 2 is the same model on a larger scale.

"As yet 3 can be of little use to us. It includes a room 13 feet by 11. X is the windows and other apertures; and these being closed up and the subjects admitted, all that remains to be done is to lock the door from the outside and turn on the gas. E, F, and K are couches, and L is a square inch of glass through which results may be noted.

"The speciality of 4, which is called the 'water cure,' is that it is only workable on water. It is generally admitted that release by drowning is the pleasantest of all deaths; and, indeed, 4, speaking roughly, is a boat with a hole in the bottom. It is so simple that a child could work it. C is the plug.

"No. 5 is an intricate instrument. The advantage claimed for it is that it enables a large number of persons to leave together."

While the thesis was under discussion, the attendance was increased by a few members specially interested in the question of female suffrage. Andrew observed that several of these wrote something on a piece of paper which lay on the table with a pencil beside it, before taking their seats.

He stretched himself in the direction of this paper, but subsided as he caught the eyes of two of the company riveted on his neck.

From that time until he left the rooms one member or other was staring at his neck. Andrew looked anxiously in the glass over the mantelpiece but could see nothing wrong.

The paper on the table merely contained such jottings as these:--

"Robert Buchanan has written another play."

"Schnadhörst is in town."

"Ashmead Bartlett walks in Temple Gardens 3 to 4."

"Clement Scott (?)"

"Query: Is there a dark passage near Hyndman's (Socialist's) house?"

"Talmage. Address, Midland Hotel."

"Andrew Lang (?)"

Andrew was a good deal interested in woman's suffrage, and the debate on this question in the students' society at Edinburgh, when he spoke for an hour and five minutes, is still remembered by the janitor who had to keep the door until the meeting closed.

Debating societies, like the company of reporters, engender a familiarity of reference to eminent persons, and Andrew had in his time struck down the champions of woman's rights as a boy plays with his ninepins.

To be brought face to face with a lady whose name is a household word wheresoever a few Scotchmen can meet and resolve themselves into an argument was another matter.

It was with no ordinary mingling of respect with curiosity that he stood up with the others to greet Mrs. Fawcett as the president led her into the room. The young man's face, as he looked upon her for the first time, was the best book this remarkable woman ever wrote.

The proceedings were necessarily quiet, and the president had introduced their guest to the meeting without Andrew's hearing a word.

He was far away in a snow-swept University quadrangle on a windy night, when Mrs. Fawcett rose to her feet.

Some one flung open the window, for the place was close, and immediately the skirl of a bagpiper broke the silence.

It might have been the devil that rushed into the room.

Still Andrew dreamed on.

The guest paused.

The members looked at each other, and the president nodded to one of them.

He left the room, and about two minutes afterwards the music suddenly ceased.

Andrew woke with a start in time to see him return, write two words in the members' book, and resume his seat. Mrs. Fawcett then began.

"I have before me," she said, turning over the leaves of a bulky manuscript, "a great deal of matter bearing on the question of woman's rights, which at such a meeting as this may be considered read. It is mainly historical, and while I am prepared to meet with hostile criticism from the society, I assume that the progress our agitation has made, with its disappointments, its trials, and its triumphs, has been followed more or less carefully by you all.

"Nor shall I, after the manner of speakers on such an occasion, pay you the doubtful compliment of fulsomely extolling your aims before your face.

"I come at once to the question of woman's rights in so far as the society can affect them, and I ask of you a consideration of my case with as little prejudice as men can be expected to approach it.

"In the constitution of the society, as it has been explained to me, I notice chiefly two things which would have filled me with indignation twenty years ago, but only remind me how far we are from the goal of our ambition now.

"The first is a sin of omission, the second one of commission, and the latter is the more to be deprecated in that you made it with your eyes open, after full discussion, while the other came about as a matter of course.

"I believe I am right in saying that the membership of this society is exclusively male, and also that no absolute veto has been placed on female candidature.

"As a matter of fact, it never struck the founders that such a veto in black and white was necessary. When they drew up the rules of membership the other sex never fell like a black shadow on the paper; it was forgotten. We owe our eligibility to many other offices (generally disputed at law) to the same accident. In short, the unwritten law of the argumentum ad crinolinam puts us to the side."

Having paid the society the compliment of believing that, however much it differed from her views, it would not dismiss them with a laugh, Mrs. Fawcett turned to the question of woman's alleged physical limitations.

She said much on this point that Andrew saw could not be easily refuted, but, interesting though she made it, we need not follow her over beaten ground.

So far the members had given her the courteous non-attention which thoughtful introductory remarks can always claim. It was when she reached her second head that they fastened upon her words.

Then Andrew had seen no sharper audience since he was one of a Scotch congregation on the scent of a heretic.

"At a full meeting of committee," said Mrs. Fawcett, with a ring of bitterness in her voice, "you passed a law that women should not enjoy the advantages of the association. Be they ever so eminent, their sex deprives them of your care. You take up the case of a petty maker of books because his tea-leaf solutions weary you, and you put a stop to him with an enthusiasm worthy of a nobler object.

"But the woman is left to decay.

"This society at its noblest was instituted for taking strong means to prevent men's slipping down the ladder it has been such a toil to them to mount, but the women who have climbed as high as they can fall from rung to rung.

"There are female nuisances as well as male; I presume no one here will gainsay me that. But you do not know them officially. The politicians who joke about three acres and a cow, the writers who are comic about mothers-in-law, the very boot-blacks have your solicitude, but you ignore their complements in the softer sex.

"Yet you call yourselves a society for suppressing excrescences! Your president tells me you are at present inquiring for the address of the man who signs himself 'Paterfamilias' in the 'Times'; but the letters from 'A British Matron' are of no account.

"I do not need to be told how Dr. Smith, the fashionable physician, was precipitated down that area the other day; but what I do ask is, why should he be taken and all the lady doctors left?

"Their degrees are as good as his. You are too 'manly,' you say, to arrest their course. Is injustice manliness? We have another name for it. We say you want the pluck.

"I suppose every one of you has been reading a very able address recently delivered at the meeting of the Social Science Congress. I refer to my friend Mrs. Kendal's paper on the moral aspect of the drama in this country.

"It is a powerful indictment of the rank and file other professional brothers and sisters, and nowhere sadder, more impressive, or more unanswerable than where she speaks of the involuntary fall of the actor into social snobbishness and professional clap-trap.

"I do not know how the paper affected you. But since reading it I have asked in despair, how can this gifted lady continue to pick her way between the snares with which the stage is beset?

"Is it possible that the time may come when she will advertise by photographs and beg from reporters the 'pars' she now so scathingly criticises? Nay, when I look upon the drop scene at the St. James's Theatre, I ask myself if the deterioration has not already set in.

"Gentlemen, is this a matter of indifference to you? But why do I ask? Has not Mrs. Lynn Linton another article in the new 'Nineteenth Century' that makes her worthy your attention? They are women, and the sex is outside your sphere."

It was nearly twelve o'clock when Mrs. Fawcett finished her address, and the society had adopted the good old rule of getting to bed betimes. Thus it was afterwards that Andrew learned how long and carefully the society had already considered the advisability of giving women equal rights with men.

As he was leaving the chambers the president slipped something into his hand. He held it there until he reached his room.

On the way a man struck against him, scanned him piercingly, and then shuffled off. He was muffled up, but Andrew wondered if he had not seen him at the meeting.

The young Scotchman had an uneasy feeling that his footsteps were dodged.

As soon as he reached home he unfolded the scrap of paper that had been pushed into his hand. It merely contained these words--

"Cover up your neck."

CHAPTER V

On the following Tuesday Andrew met the president by appointment at the Marble Arch.

Until he had received his final instructions he was pledged not to begin, and he had passed these two intervening days staring at his empty fireplace.

They shook hands silently and passed into the Park. The president was always thoughtful in a crowd.

"In such a gathering as this," said Andrew, pointing an imaginary pistol at a lecturer on Socialism, "you could hardly go wrong to let fly."

"You must not speak like that," the president said gently, "or we shall soon lose you. Your remark, however, opens the way for what I have to say. You have never expressed any curiosity as to your possible fate. I hope this is not because you under-estimate the risks. If the authorities saw you 'letting fly' as you term it, promiscuously, or even at a given object, they would treat you as no better than a malefactor."

"I thought that all out yesterday," said Andrew, "and I am amazed at the society's success in escaping detection."

"I feared this," said the president. "You are mistaken. We don't always escape detection. Sometimes we are caught--"

"Caught?"

"Yes, and hanged."

"But if that is so, why does it not get into the papers?"

"The papers are full of it."

Andrew looked incredulous.

"In the present state of the law," said the president, "motive in a murder goes for nothing. However iniquitous this may be--and I do not attempt to defend it--we accept it as a fact. Your motives may have been unexceptionable, but they hang you all the same. Thus our members when apprehended preserve silence on this point, or say that they are Fenians. This is to save the society. The man who got fifteen years the other day for being found near St. Stephen's with six infernal machines in his pockets was really one of us. He was taking them to be repaired."

"And the other who got ten years the week before?"

"He was from America, but it was for one of our affairs that he was sentenced. He was quite innocent. You see the dynamiters, vulgarly so called, are playing into our hands. Suspicion naturally falls on them. He was our fifth."

"I had no idea of this," murmured Andrew.

"You see what a bad name does," said the president. "Let this be a warning to you, Andrew."

"But is this quite fair?"

"As for that, they like it--the leading spirits, I mean. It gives them a reputation. Besides, they hurt as well as help us. It was after their appearance that the authorities were taught to be distrustful. You have little idea of the precautions taken nowadays. There is Sir William Harcourt, for instance, who is attended by policemen everywhere. I used to go home from the House behind him nightly, but I could never get him alone. I have walked in the very shadow of that man, but always in a company."

"You were never arrested yourself?" asked Andrew.

"I was once, but we substituted a probationer."

"Then did he--was he--"

"Yes, poor fellow."

"Is that often done?"

"Sometimes. You perhaps remember the man who went over the Embankment the night we met? Well, if I had been charged with that, you would have had to be hanged."

Andrew took a seat to collect his thoughts.

"Was that why you seemed to take to me so much?" he asked, wistfully.

"It was only one reason," said the president, soothingly. "I liked you from the first."

"But I don't see," said Andrew, "why I should have suffered for your action."

For the moment, his veneration for this remarkable man hung in the balance.

"It would have been for the society's sake," said the president, simply; "probationers are hardly missed."

His face wore a pained look, but there was no reproach in his voice.

Andrew was touched.

He looked the apology, which, as a Scotchman, he could not go the length of uttering.

"Before I leave you to-day," said the president, turning to a pleasanter subject, "I shall give you some money. We do not, you understand, pay our probationers a fixed salary."

"It is more, is it not," said Andrew, "in nature of a scholarship?"

"Yes, a scholarship--for the endowment of research. You see we do not tie you down to any particular line of study. Still, I shall be happy to hear of any programme you may have drawn up."

Andrew hesitated. He did not know that, to the president, he was an open book.

"I dare say I can read your thoughts," said his companion. "There is an eminent person whom you would like to make your first?"

Andrew admitted that this was so.

"I do not ask any confidences of you," continued the president, "nor shall I discourage ambition. But I hope, Andrew, you have only in view the greatest good of the greatest number. At such a time, it is well for the probationer to ask himself two questions: Is it not self-glorification that prompts me to pick this man out from among so many? and, Am I actuated by any personal animosity? If you cannot answer both these questions in the negative, it is time to ask a third, Should I go on with this undertaking?"

"In this case," said Andrew, "I do not think it is self-glory, and I am sure it is not spite. He is a man I have a very high opinion of."

"A politician? Remember that we are above party considerations."

"He is a politician," said Andrew, reluctantly, "but it is his politics I admire."

"And you are sure his time has come? Then how do you propose to set about it?"

"I thought of calling at his house, and putting it to him."

The president's countenance fell.

"Well, well," he said, "that may answer. But there is no harm in bearing in mind that persuasion is not necessarily a passive force. Without going the length of removing him yourself, you know, you could put temptation in his way."

"If I know my man," said Andrew, "that will not be required."

The president had drunk life's disappointments to the dregs, but it was not in his heart to damp the youth's enthusiasm.

Experience he knew to be a commodity for which we pay a fancy price.

"After that," said Andrew, "I thought of Henry Irving."

"We don't kill actors," his companion said.

It was Andrew's countenance's turn to fall now.

"We don't have time for it," the president explained. "When the society was instituted, we took a few of them, but merely to get our hands in. We didn't want to bungle good cases, you see, and it did not matter so much for them."

"How did you do it?"

"We waited at the stage-door, and went off with the first person who came out, male or female."

"But I understood you did not take up women?"

"Nor do we. Theatrical people constitute a sex by themselves--like curates."

"Then can't I even do the man who stands at the theatre doors, all shirt-front and diamonds?"

The president shivered.

"If you happen to be passing, at any rate," he said.

"And surely some of the playwrights would be better dead. They must see that themselves."

"They have had their chance," said the president. Despite his nationality, Andrew had not heard the story, so the president told it him.

"Many years ago, when the drama was in its infancy, some young men from Stratford-on-Avon and elsewhere resolved to build a theatre in London.

"The times, however, were moral, and no one would imperil his soul so far as to give them a site.

"One night, they met in despair, when suddenly the room was illumined by lightning, and they saw the devil in the midst of them.

"He has always been a large proprietor in London, and he had come to strike a bargain with them. They could have as many sites as they chose, on one condition. Every year they must send him a dramatist.

"You see he was willing to take his chance of the players.

"The compact was made, and up to the present time it has been religiously kept. But this year, as the day drew near, found the managers very uneasy. They did what they could. They forwarded the best man they had."

"What happened?" asked Andrew, breathlessly.

"The devil sent him back," said the president.

CHAPTER VI

It was one Sunday forenoon, on such a sunny day as slovenly men seize upon to wash their feet and have it over, that Andrew set out to call on Mr. Labouchere.

The leaves in the squares were green, and the twittering of the birds among the boughs was almost gay enough to charm him out of the severity of countenance which a Scotchman wears on a Sunday with his blacks.

Andrew could not help regarding the mother-of-pearl sky as a favourable omen. Several times he caught himself becoming light-hearted.

He got the great Radical on the door-step, just setting out for church.

The two men had not met before, but Andrew was a disciple in the school in which the other taught.

Between man and man formal introductions are humbug.

Andrew explained in a few words the nature of his visit, and received a cordial welcome.

"But I could call again," he said, observing the hymn-book in the other's hand.

"Nonsense," said Mr. Labouchere heartily; "it must be business before pleasure. Mind the step."

So saying, he led his visitor into a cheerful snuggery at the back of the house. It was furnished with a careful contempt for taste, and the first thing that caught Andrew's eye was a pot of apple jam on a side table.

"I have no gum," Mr. Labouchere explained hastily.

A handsomely framed picture, representing Truth lying drowned at the bottom of a well, stood on the mantel-piece; indeed, there were many things in the room that, on another occasion, Andrew would have been interested to hear the history of.

He could not but know, however, that at present he was to some extent an intruder, and until he had fully explained his somewhat delicate business he would not feel at ease.

Though argumentative, Andrew was essentially a shy, proud man.

It was very like Mr. Labouchere to leave him to tell his story in his own way, only now and then, at the outset, interjecting a humorous remark, which we here omit.

"I hope," said Andrew earnestly, "that you will not think it fulsome on my part to say how much I like you. In your public utterances you have let it be known what value you set on pretty phrases; but I speak the blunt truth, as you have taught it. I am only a young man, perhaps awkward and unpolished--"

Here Andrew paused, but as Mr. Labouchere did not say anything he resumed.

"That as it may be, I should like you to know that your political speeches have become part of my life. When I was a student it seemed to me that the Radicalism of so called advanced thinkers was a half-hearted sham; I had no interest in politics at all until I read your attack--one of them--on the House of Lords. That day marked an epoch in my life. I used to read the University library copy of 'Truth' from cover to cover. Sometimes I carried it into the class-room. That was not allowed. I took it up my waistcoat. In those days I said that if I wrote a book I would dedicate it to you without permission, and London, when I came to it, was to me the town where you lived."

There was a great deal of truth in this; indeed, Mr. Labouchere's single-hearted enthusiasm--be his politics right or wrong--is well calculated to fascinate young men.

If it was slightly over-charged, the temptation was great. Andrew was keenly desirous of carrying his point, and he wanted his host to see that he was only thinking of his good.

"Well, but what is it you would have me do?" asked Mr. Labouchere, who often had claimants on his bounty and his autographs.

"I want you," said Andrew eagerly, "to die."

The two men looked hard at each other. There was not even a clock in the room to break the silence. At last the statesman spoke.

"Why?" he asked.

His visitor sank back in his chair relieved. He had put all his hopes in the other's common-sense.

It had never failed Mr. Labouchere, and now it promised not to fail Andrew.

"I am anxious to explain that," the young man said glibly. "If you can look at yourself with the same eyes with which you see other people, it won't take long. Make a looking-glass of me, and it is done.

"You have now reached a high position in the worlds of politics and literature, to which you have cut your way unaided.

"You are a great satirist, combining instruction with amusement, a sort of comic Carlyle.

"You hate shams so much that if man had been constructed for it I dare say you would kick at yourself.

"You have your enemies, but the very persons who blunt their weapons on you do you the honour of sharpening them on 'Truth.' In short, you have reached the summit of your fame, and you are too keen a man of the world not to know that fame is a touch-and-go thing."

Andrew paused.

"Go on," said Mr. Labouchere.

"Well, you have now got fame, honour, everything for which it is legitimate in man to strive.

"So far back as I can remember, you have had the world laughing with you. But you know what human nature is.

"There comes a morning to all wits, when their public wakes to find them bores. The fault may not be the wit's, but what of that? The result is the same.

"Wits are like theatres: they may have a glorious youth and prime, but their old age is dismal. To the outsider, like myself, signs are not wanting--to continue the figure of speech--that you have put on your last successful piece.

"Can you say candidly that your last Christmas number was more than a reflection of its predecessors, or that your remarks this year on the Derby day took as they did the year before?

"Surely the most incisive of our satirists will not let himself degenerate into an illustration of Mr. Herbert Spencer's theory that man repeats himself, like history.

"Mr. Labouchere, sir, to those of us who have grown up in your inspiration it would indeed be pitiful if this were so."

Andrew's host turned nervously in his chair.

Probably he wished that he had gone to church now.

"You need not be alarmed," he said, with a forced smile.

"You will die," cried Andrew, "before they send you to the House of Lords?"

"In which case the gain would be all to those left behind."

"No," said Andrew, who now felt that he had as good as gained the day; "there could not be a greater mistake.

"Suppose it happened to-night, or even put it off to the end of the week; see what would follow.

"The ground you have lost so far is infinitesimal. It would be forgotten in the general regret.

"Think of the newspaper placards next morning, some of them perhaps edged with black; the leaders in every London paper and in all the prominent provincial ones; the six columns obituary in the 'Times'; the paragraphs in the 'World'; the motion by Mr. Gladstone or Mr. Healy for the adjournment of the House; the magazine articles; the promised memoirs; the publication of posthumous papers; the resolution in the Northampton Town Council; the statue in Hyde Park! With such a recompense where would be the sacrifice?"

Mr. Labouchere rose and paced the room in great mental agitation.

"Now look at the other side of the picture," said Andrew, rising and following him: "'Truth' reduced to threepence, and then to a penny; yourself confused with Tracy Turnerelli or Martin Tupper; your friends running when you looked like jesting; the House emptying, the reporters shutting their note-books as you rose to speak; the great name of Labouchere become a synonym for bore!"

They presented a strange picture in that room, its owner's face now a greyish white, his supplicant shaking with a passion that came out in perspiration.

With trembling hand Mr. Labouchere flung open the window. The room was stifling.

There was a smell of new-mown hay in the air, a gentle breeze tipped the well-trimmed hedge with life, and the walks crackled in the heat.

But a stone's throw distant the sun was bathing in the dimpled Thames.

There was a cawing of rooks among the tall trees, and a church-bell tinkled in the ivy far away across the river.

Mr. Labouchere was far away too.

He was a round-cheeked boy again, smothering his kitten in his pinafore, prattling of Red Riding Hood by his school-mistress's knee, and guddling in the brook for minnows.

And now--and now!

It was a beautiful world, and, ah, life is sweet!

He pressed his fingers to his forehead.

"Leave me," he said hoarsely.

Andrew put his hand upon the shoulder of the man he loved so well.

"Be brave," he said; "do it in whatever way you prefer. A moment's suffering, and all will be over."

He spoke gently. There is always something infinitely pathetic in the sight of a strong man in pain.

Mr. Labouchere turned upon him.

"Go," he cried, "or I will call the servants."

"You forget," said Andrew, "that I am your guest."

But his host only pointed to the door.

Andrew felt a great sinking at his heart. They prate who say it is success that tries a man. He flung himself at Mr. Labouchere's feet.

"Think of the public funeral," he cried.

His host seized the bell-rope and pulled it violently.

"If you will do it," said Andrew solemnly, "I promise to lay flowers on your grave every day till I die."

"John," said Mr. Labouchere, "show this gentleman out."

Andrew rose.

"You refuse?" he asked.

"I do."

"You won't think it over? If I call again, say on Thursday--"

"John!" said Mr. Labouchere.

Andrew took up his hat. His host thought he had gone. But in the hall his reflection in a looking-glass reminded the visitor of something. He put his head in at the doorway again.

"Would you mind telling me," he said, "whether you see anything peculiar about my neck?"

"It seems a good neck to twist," Mr. Labouchere answered, a little savagely.

Andrew then withdrew.

CHAPTER VII

This unexpected rebuff from Mr. Labouchere rankled for many days in Andrew's mind. Had he been proposing for the great statesman's hand he could not have felt it more. Perhaps he did not make sufficient allowance for Mr. Labouchere; it is always so easy to advise.

But to rage at a man (or woman) is the proof that we can adore them; it is only his loved ones who infuriate a Scotchman.

There were moments when Andrew said to himself that he had nothing more to live for.

Then he would upbraid himself for having gone about it too hurriedly, and in bitter self-contempt strike his hand on the railings, as he rushed by.

Work is the sovereign remedy for this unhealthy state of mind, and fortunately Andrew had a great deal to do.

Gradually the wound healed, and he began to take an interest in Lord Randolph Churchill.

Every day the Flying Scotchman shoots its refuse of clever young men upon London who are too ambitious to do anything.

Andrew was not one of these.

Seeking to carry off one of the greatest prizes in his profession, he had aimed too high for a beginner.

When he realised this he apprenticed himself, so to speak, to the president, determined to acquire a practical knowledge of his art in all its branches. Though a very young man, he had still much to learn. It was only in his leisure moments that he gave way to dreams over a magnum opus .

But when he did set about it, which must be before his period of probation closed, he had made up his mind to be thorough.

The months thus passed quietly but not unprofitably in assisting the president, acquainting himself with the favourite resorts of interesting persons and composing his thesis.

At intervals the monotony was relieved by more strictly society work. On these occasions he played a part not dissimilar to that of a junior counsel.

The president found him invaluable in his raid on the gentlemen with umbrellas who read newspapers in the streets.

It was Andrew--though he never got the credit of it--who put his senior in possession of the necessary particulars about the comic writers whose subject is teetotalism and spinsters.

He was unwearying, indeed, in his efforts with regard to the comic journals generally, and the first man of any note that he disposed of was "Punch's" favourite artist on Scotch matters. This was in an alley off Fleet Street.

Andrew took a new interest in the House of Lords, and had a magnificent scheme for ending it in half an hour.

As the members could never be got together in any number, this fell through.

Lord Brabourne will remember the young man in a straw hat, with his neck covered up, who attended the House so regularly when it was announced that he was to speak. That was Andrew.

It was he who excitedly asked the Black Rod to point out Lord Sherbrooke, when it was intimated that this peer was preparing a volume of poems for the press.

In a month's time Andrew knew the likeliest places to meet these and other noble lords alone.

The publishing offices of "England," the only Conservative newspaper, had a fascination for him.

He got to know Mr. Ashmead Bartlett's hours of calling, until the sight of him on the pavement was accepted as a token that the proprietor was inside.

They generally reached the House of Commons about the same time.

Here Andrew's interest was discriminated among quite a number of members. Mr. Bradlaugh, Mr. Sexton, and Mr. Marjoribanks, the respected member for Berwickshire, were perhaps his favourites; but the one he dwelt with most pride on was Lord Randolph Churchill.

One night he gloated so long over Sir George Trevelyan leaning over Westminster Bridge that in the end he missed him.

When Andrew made up his mind to have a man he got to like him. This was his danger.

With press tickets, which he got very cheap, he often looked in at the theatres to acquaint himself with the faces and figures of the constant frequenters.

He drew capital pencil sketches of the leading critics in his note-book.

The gentleman next him that night at "Manteaux Noirs" would not have laughed so heartily if he had known why Andrew listened for his address to the cabman.

The young Scotchman resented people's merriment over nothing; sometimes he took the Underground Railway just to catch clerks at "Tit-Bits."

One afternoon he saw some way in front of him in Piccadilly a man with a young head on old shoulders.

Andrew recognized him by the swing of his stick; he could have identified his plaid among a hundred thousand morning coats. It was John Stuart Blackie, his favourite professor.

Since the young man graduated, his old preceptor had resigned his chair, and was now devoting his time to writing sonnets to himself in the Scotch newspapers.

Andrew could not bear to think of it, and quickened his pace to catch him up. But Blackie was in great form, humming "Scots wha hae." With head thrown back, staff revolving and chest inflated, he sang himself into a martial ecstasy, and, drumming cheerily on the doors with his fist, strutted along like a band of bagpipers with a clan behind him, until he had played himself out of Andrew's sight.

Far be it from our intention to maintain that Andrew was invariably successful. That is not given to any man.

Sometimes his hands slipped.

Had he learned the piano in his younger days this might not have happened. But if he had been a pianist the president would probably have wiped him out--and very rightly. There can be no doubt about male pianists.

Nor was the fault always Andrew's. When the society was founded, many far-seeing men had got wind of it, and had themselves elected honorary members before the committee realised what they were after.

This was a sore subject with the president; he shunned discussing it, and thus Andrew had frequently to discontinue cases after he was well on with them.

In this way much time was lost.

Andrew was privately thanked by the committee for one suggestion, which, for all he knows, may yet be carried out. The president had a wide interest in the press, and on one occasion he remarked to Andrew:

"Think of the snobs and the prigs who would be saved if the 'Saturday Review' and the 'Spectator' could be induced to cease publication!"

Andrew thought it out, and then produced his scheme.

The battle of the clans on the North Inch of Perth had always seemed to him a master-stroke of diplomacy.

"Why," he said to the president, "not set the 'Saturday's' staff against the 'Spectator's.' If about equally matched, they might exterminate each other."

So his days of probation passed, and the time drew nigh for Andrew to show what stuff was in him.

CHAPTER VIII

Andrew had set apart July 31 for killing Lord Randolph Churchill.

As his term of probation was up in the second week of August, this would leave him nearly a fortnight to finish his thesis in.

On the 30th he bought a knife in Holborn suitable for his purpose. It had been his original intention to use an electric rifle, but those he was shown were too cumbrous for use in the streets.

The eminent statesman was residing at this time at the Grand Hotel, and Andrew thought to get him somewhere between Trafalgar Square and the House. Taking up his position in a window of Morley's Hotel at an early hour, he set himself to watch the windows opposite. The plan of the Grand was well known to him, for he had frequently made use of it as overlooking the National Liberal Club, whose membership he had already slightly reduced.

Turning his eyes to the private sitting-rooms, he soon discovered Lord Randolph busily writing in one of them.

Andrew had lunch at Morley's, so that he might be prepared for any emergency. Lord Randolph wrote on doggedly through the forenoon, and Andrew hoped he would finish what he was at in case this might be his last chance.

It rained all through the afternoon. The thick drizzle seemed to double the width of the street, and even to Andrew's strained eyes the shadow in the room opposite was obscured.

His eyes wandered from the window to the hotel entrance, and as cab after cab rattled from it he became uneasy.

In ordinary circumstances he could have picked his man out anywhere, but in rain all men look alike. He could have dashed across the street and rushed from room to room of the Grand Hotel.

His self-restraint was rewarded.

Late in the afternoon Lord Randolph came to the window. The flashing waterproofs and scurrying umbrellas were a surprise to him, and he knitted his brows in annoyance.

By-and-by his face was convulsed with laughter.

He drew a chair to the window and stood on it, that he might have a better view of the pavement beneath.

For some twenty minutes he remained there smacking his thighs, his shoulders heaving with glee.

Andrew could not see what it was, but he formulated a theory.

Heavy blobs of rain that had gathered on the window-sill slowly released their hold from time to time and fell with a plump on the hats of passers-by. Lord Randolph was watching them.

Just as they were letting go he shook the window to make the wayfarers look up. They got the rain-drops full in the face, and then he screamed.

About six o'clock Andrew paid his bill hurriedly and ran downstairs. Lord Randolph had come to the window in his greatcoat. His follower waited for him outside. It was possible that he would take a hansom and drive straight to the House, but Andrew had reasons for thinking this unlikely. The rain had somewhat abated. Lord Randolph came out, put up his umbrella, and, glancing at the sky for a moment, set off briskly up St. Martin's Lane.

Andrew knew that he would not linger here, for they had done St. Martin's Lane already.

Lord Randolph's movements these last days had excited the Scotchman's curiosity. He had been doing the London streets systematically during his unoccupied afternoons. But it was difficult to discover what he was after.

It was the tobacconists' shops that attracted him.

He did not enter, only stood at the windows counting something.

He jotted down the result on a piece of paper and then sped on to the next shop.

In this way, with Andrew at his heels, he had done the whole of the W. C. district, St. James's, Oxford Street, Piccadilly, Bond Street, and the Burlington Arcade.

On this occasion he took the small thoroughfares lying between upper Regent Street and Tottenham Court Road. Beginning in Great Titchfield Street he went from tobacconist's to tobacconist's, sometimes smiling to himself, at other times frowning. Andrew scrutinised the windows as he left them, but could make nothing of it.

Not for the first time he felt that there could be no murder to-night unless he saw the paper first.

Lord Randolph devoted an hour to this work. Then he hailed a cab.

Andrew expected this. But the statesman still held the paper loosely in his hand.

It was a temptation.

Andrew bounded forward as if to open the cab door, pounced upon the paper and disappeared with it up an alley. After five minutes' dread lest he might be pursued, he struck a match and read:

"Great Titchfield Street--Branscombe 15, Churchill 11, Langtry 8, Gladstone 4.

"Mortimer Street--Langtry 11, Branscombe 9, Gladstone 6, Mary Anderson 6, Churchill 3.

"Margaret Street--Churchill 7, Anderson 6, Branscombe 5, Gladstone 4, Chamberlain 4.

"Smaller streets--Churchill 14, Branscombe 13, Gladstone 9, Langtry 9. Totals for to-day: Churchill 35, Langtry 28, Gladstone 23, Branscombe 42, Anderson 12, Chamberlain nowhere." Then followed, as if in a burst of passion, "Branscombe still leading--confound her."

Andrew saw that Lord Randolph had been calculating fame from vesta boxes.

For a moment this discovery sent Andrew's mind wandering. Miss Branscombe's photographs obstructed the traffic. Should not this be put a stop to? Ah, but she was a woman!

This recalled him to himself. Lord Randolph had departed, probably for St. Stephen's.

Andrew jumped into a hansom. He felt like an exotic in a glass frame.

"The House," he said.

What a pity his mother could not have seen him then!

Perhaps Andrew was prejudiced. Undoubtedly he was in a mood to be easily pleased.

In his opinion at any rate. Lord Randolph's speech that night on the Irish question was the best he ever delivered.

It came on late in the evening, and he stuck to his text like a clergyman. He quoted from Hansard to prove that Mr. Gladstone did not know what he was talking about; he blazed out against the Parnellites till they were called to order. The ironical members who cried "Hear, hear," regretted it.

He had never been wittier, never more convincing, never so magnificently vituperative.

Andrew was lifted out of himself. He jumped in ecstasy to his feet. It was he who led the applause.

He felt that this was a worthy close to a brilliant career.

We oldsters looking on more coolly could have seen where the speech was lacking, so far as Andrew was concerned. It is well known that when a great man, of whom there will be biographers, is to die a violent death, his last utterances are strangely significant, as if he foresaw his end.

There was nothing of this in Lord Randolph's speech.

The House was thinning when the noble lord rose to go. Andrew joined him at the gate.

The Scotchman's nervous elation had all gone. A momentary thrill passed through his veins as he remembered that in all probability they would never be together again. After that he was quite calm.

The night was black.

The rain had ceased, but for an occasional drop shaken out of a shivering star.

But for a few cabs rolling off with politicians, Whitehall was deserted.

The very tax-collectors seemed to have got to bed.

Lord Randolph shook hands with two or three other members homeward bound, walked a short distance with one of them, and then set off towards his hotel alone.

His pace was leisurely, as that of a man in profound thought.

There was no time to be lost; but Andrew dallied.

Once he crept up and could have done it. He thought he would give him another minute. There was a footstep behind, and he fell back. It was Sir William Harcourt. Lord Randolph heard him, and, seeing who it was, increased his pace.

The illustrious Liberal slackened at the same moment.

Andrew bit his lip and hurried on.

Some time was lost in getting round Sir William.

He was advancing in strides now.

Lord Randolph saw that he was pursued.

When Andrew began to run, he ran too.

There were not ten yards between them at Whitehall Place.

A large man turning the corner of Great Scotland Yard fell against Andrew. He was wheeled aside, but Mr. Chaplin had saved a colleague's life.

With a cry Andrew bounded on, his knife glistening.

Trafalgar Square was a black mass.

Lord Randolph took Northumberland Avenue in four steps, Andrew almost on the top of him.

As he burst through the door of the Grand Hotel, his pursuer made one tremendous leap, and his knife catching Lord Randolph in the heel, carried away his shoe.

Andrew's face had struck the steps.

He heard the word "Fenian."

There was a rushing to and fro of lights.

Springing to his feet, he thrust the shoe into his pocket and went home.

CHAPTER IX

"Tie this muffler round your neck."

It was the president who spoke. Andrew held his thesis in his hand.

"But the rooms are so close," he said.

"That has nothing to do with it," said the president. The blood rushed to his head, and then left him pale.

"But why?" asked Andrew.

"For God's sake, do as I bid you," said his companion, pulling himself by a great effort to the other side of the room.

"You have done it?" he asked, carefully avoiding Andrew's face.

"Yes, but--"

"Then we can go in to the others. Remember what I told you about omitting the first seven pages. The society won't stand introductory remarks in a thesis."

The committee were assembled in the next room.

When the young Scotchman entered with the president, they looked him full in the neck.

"He is suffering from cold," the president said.

No one replied, but angry eyes were turned on the speaker. He somewhat nervously placed his young friend in a bad light, with a table between him and his hearers.

Then Andrew began.

"The Society for Doing Without," he read, "has been tried and found wanting. It has now been in existence for some years, and its members have worked zealously, though unostentatiously.

"I am far from saying a word against them. They are patriots as true as ever petitioned against the Channel Tunnel."

"No compliments," whispered the president, warningly. Andrew hastily turned a page, and continued:

"But what have they done? Removed an individual here and there. That is the extent of it.

"You have been pursuing a half-hearted policy. You might go on for centuries at this rate before you made any perceptible difference in the streets.

"Have you ever seen a farmer thinning turnips? Gentlemen, there is an example for you. My proposal is that everybody should have to die on reaching the age of forty-five years.

"It has been the wish of this society to avoid the prejudices engendered of party strife. But though you are a social rather than a political organisation, you cannot escape politics. You do not call yourselves Radicals, but you work for Radicalism. What is Radicalism? It is a desire to get a chance. This is an aspiration inherent in the human breast. It is felt most keenly by the poor.

"Make the poor rich, and the hovels, the misery, the immorality, and the crime of the East End disappear. It is infamous, say the Socialists, that this is not done at once. Yes, but how is it to be done? Not, as they hold, by making the classes and the masses change places. Not on the lines on which the society has hitherto worked. There is only one way, and I make it my text to-night. Fortunately, it presents no considerable difficulties.

"It is well known in medicine that the simplest--in other words, the most natural--remedies may be the most efficacious.

"So it is in the social life. What shall we do, Society asks, with our boys? I reply. Kill off the parents.

"There can be little doubt that forty-five years is long enough for a man to live. Parents must see that. Youth is the time to have your fling.

"Let us see how this plan would revolutionise the world. It would make statesmen hurry up. At present, they are nearly fifty before you hear of them. How can we expect the country to be properly governed by men in their dotage?

"Again, take the world of letters. Why does the literary aspirant have such a struggle? Simply because the profession is over-stocked with seniors. I would like to know what Tennyson's age is, and Ruskin's, and Browning's. Every one of them is over seventy, and all writing away yet as lively as you like. It is a crying scandal.

"Things are the same in medicine, art, divinity, law--in short, in every profession and in every trade.

"Young ladies cry out that this is not a marrying age. How can it be a marrying age, with grey-headed parents everywhere? Give young men their chance, and they will marry younger than ever, if only to see their children grown up before they die.

"A word in conclusion. Looking around me, I cannot but see that most, if not all, of my hearers have passed what should plainly be the allotted span of life to man. You would have to go.

"But, gentlemen, you would do so feeling that you were setting a noble example. Younger, and--may I say?--more energetic men would fill your places and carry on your work. You would hardly be missed."

Andrew rolled up his thesis blandly, and strode into the next room to await the committee's decision. It cannot be said that he felt the slightest uneasiness.

The president followed, shutting the door behind him.

"You have just two minutes," he said.

Andrew could not understand it.

His hat was crushed on to his head, his coat flung at him; he was pushed out at a window, squeezed through a grating and tumbled into a passage.

"What is the matter?" he asked, as the president dragged him down a back street.

The president pointed to the window they had just left.

Half a dozen infuriated men were climbing from it in pursuit. Their faces, drunk with rage, awoke Andrew to a sense of his danger.

"They were drawing lots for you when I left the room," said the president.

"But what have I done?" gasped Andrew.

"They didn't like your thesis. At least, they make that their excuse."

"Excuse?"

"Yes; it was really your neck that did it."

By this time they were in a cab, rattling into Gray's Inn Road.

"They are a poor lot," said Andrew fiercely, "if they couldn't keep their heads over my neck."

"They are only human," retorted the president. "For Heaven's sake, pull up the collar of your coat."

His fingers were itching, but Andrew did not notice it.

"Where are we going?" he asked.

"To King's Cross. The midnight express leaves in twenty minutes. It is your last chance."

Andrew was in a daze. When the president had taken his ticket for Glasgow he was still groping.

The railway officials probably thought him on his honeymoon.

They sauntered along the platform beyond the lights.

Andrew, who was very hot, unloosened his greatcoat.

In a moment a great change came over his companion. All the humanity went from his face, his whole figure shook, and it was only by a tremendous effort that he chained his hands to his side.

"Your neck," he cried; "cover it up."

Andrew did not understand. He looked about him for the committee.

"There are none of them here," he said feebly.

The president had tried to warn him.

Now he gave way.

The devil that was in him leapt at Andrew's throat.

The young Scotchman was knocked into a goods waggon, with the president twisted round him.

At that moment there was heard the whistle of the Scotch express.

"Your blood be on your own head," cried the president, yielding completely to temptation.

His fingers met round the young man's neck.

"My God!" he murmured, in a delirious ecstasy, "what a neck, what a neck!"

Just then his foot slipped.

He fell. Andrew jumped up and kicked him as hard as he could three times.

Then he leapt to the platform, and, flinging himself into the moving train, fell exhausted on the seat.

Andrew never thought so much of the president again. You cannot respect a man and kick him.

CHAPTER X

The first thing Andrew did on reaching Wheens was to write to his London landlady to send on his box with clothes by goods train; also his tobacco pouch, which he had left on the mantelpiece, and two pencils which she would find in the tea-caddy.

Then he went around to the manse.

The minister had great news for him.

The master of the Wheens Grammar School had died. Andrew had only to send in his testimonials, and the post was his.

The salary was 200 pounds per annum, with an assistant and the privilege of calling himself rector.

This settled, Andrew asked for Clarrie. He was humbler now than he had been, and in our disappointments we turn to woman for solace.

Clarrie had been working socks for him, and would have had them finished by this time had she known how to turn the heel.

It is his sweetheart a man should be particular about. Once he settles down it does not much matter whom he marries.

All this and much more the good old minister pointed out to Andrew. Then he left Clarrie and her lover together.

The winsome girl held one of the socks on her knee--who will chide her?--and a tear glistened in her eye.

Andrew was a good deal affected.

"Clarrie," he said softly, "will you be my wife?"

She clung to him in reply. He kissed her fondly.

"Clarrie, beloved," he said nervously, after a long pause, "how much are seven and thirteen?"

"Twenty-three," said Clarrie, putting up her mouth to his.

Andrew laughed a sad vacant laugh.

He felt that he would never understand a woman. But his fingers wandered through her tobacco-coloured hair.

He had a strange notion.

"Put your arms round my neck," he whispered.

Thus the old, old story was told once more.

A month afterwards the president of the Society for Doing Without received by post a box of bride-cake, adorned with the silver gilt which is also largely used for coffins.

* * * * * *

More than two years have passed since Andrew's marriage, and already the minister has two sweet grandchildren, in whom he renews his youth.

Except during school-hours their parents' married life is one long honeymoon.

Clarrie has put Lord Randolph Churchill's shoe into a glass case on the piano, and, as is only natural, Andrew is now a staunch Conservative.

Domesticated and repentant, he has renounced the devil and all her works.

Sometimes, when thinking of the past, the babble of his lovely babies jars upon him, and, still half-dreaming, he brings their heads close together.

At such a time all the anxious mother has to say is:

"Andrew!"

Then with a start he lays them gently in a heap on the floor, and, striding the room, soon regains his composure.

For Andrew has told Clarrie all the indiscretions of his life in London, and she has forgiven everything.

Ah, what will not a wife forgive!